For Miranda and Euan, with love
— S.P.

For Chris P. with love
— M.M.

Text copyright © 2002 by Simon Puttoc
Illustrations copyright © 2002 by Mary McC

First U.S. Edition
First published in the United Kingdom in
by Bodley Head Children's Books, Random

ISBN 0-316-78816-3
LCCN 2001092468

10 9 8 7 6 5 4 3 2 1

Printed in Singapore

The text was set in Carré Noire

# Squeaky Clean

by Simon Puttock

Illustrated by Mary McQuillan

 **LITTLE, BROWN AND COMPANY**
Boston   New York   London

Mama Pig had three little piglets, and
when they were new, they were all clean
and beautiful. But, being piglets, they
soon got grubby.

"Oh, you mucky piglets," said Mama Pig.
"Tonight you will all have a bath."

"No, no, NO!" squealed the three little piglets.
"We do not WANT to be clean!"

"Yes, yes, YES!" said Mama Pig firmly. "You are three little sillies, and you need to be scrubbed."

And she scooped them all up and popped them into the tub. But . . .

"It's too deep," squealed Piglet One.
"It's too WET!" squealed Piglet Two.
"Eek, EEK, EEK!" squealed Piglet Three.

And they squirmed and they wormed and they would NOT be washed.

"I think," said Mama Pig, "that this bath needs some . . .

bubbles!" And she swished and she swashed and she made lots of froth.

"Oooh, bubbles are pretty," said Piglet One.
"Bubbles are tickly," said Piglet Two.
"Hee, hee, hee!" said Piglet Three.
"Now," said Mama Pig, "it's time for . . .

ducks." And plop, plop, plop, three
rubber ducks dropped into the tub.

plop

plop

plop

"I like ducks," said Piglet One.

"Ducks are fun," said Piglet Two.
"Quack, quack, quack!" said Piglet Three.

"And NOW," said Mama Pig, "for . . .

splishy splashy sploshy." And she splooshed and she swooshed and galooshed them all over.

"More, more, more!" said Piglet One.
"Please sploosh ME!" said Piglet Two.
"Wheeeeeeee!" said Piglet Three. And he wriggled and he giggled and he piggled with glee.
It was the best bathtime ever.

Mama Pig dried them and kissed them and patted their heads.

"Time for bed, my piglets," she said, and she popped them in between the sheets.

"And NOW," said Mama Pig to herself,
"it is MY bathtime."

Mama Pig had LOTS of bubbles, and rubber ducks, and a soft, green scrub brush.

Then she toweled,

and powdered,

and when she was done,
she opened the door,
and there she saw . . .

her three little piglets, all clean and beautiful,
sneak, sneak, sneaking down the hall.
"Just where do you think you're going?" asked
Mama Pig.

"We are going to get GRUBBY again!" they squealed.

"Oh, you BAD, NAUGHTY piglets," said Mama Pig,
"I just got you beautiful and clean."

"We know," agreed the piglets. "We are all clean and beautiful, and we like that a lot. But we want you to give us another bath, because baths are the BEST FUN EVER!"

Mama Pig laughed and laughed.
"Oh, you GOOD little piglets, you CAN have
another bath, but two in one day is just too much.
You will all have
another tomorrow."
And she scooted
them back
to bed.

"Good night, piglets," whispered Mama Pig.

"Good night, Mama,"
said Piglet One.

"Good night, Mama,"
said Piglet Two.

But there wasn't a peep from Piglet Three,
because Piglet Three was . . .

Hee! Hee! Hee!
... splish splash sploshing all over again!